the Giving Box

the Giving Box

By Fred Rogers

RUNNING PRESS

PHILADELPHIA • LONDON

9   8   7   6   5   4   3
Digit on the right indicates the number of this printing

Library of Congress Cataloging-in-Publication Number 00-132688

ISBN 0-7624-0825-1

Cover and interior illustrations by Jennifer Herbert
Cover and interior design by Terry Peterson
Edited by Patty Aitken Smith
Concept for *The Giving Box* by Toby Schmidt
Typography: Minister, Spumoni

This book may be ordered by mail from the publisher. Please include $2.50
for postage and handling.
But try your bookstore first!

Running Press Book Publishers
125 South Twenty-second Street
Philadelphia, Pennsylvania 19103-4399

Visit us on the web!
www.runningpress.com

Contents

About Giving and Gratitude

Fred Rogers' Message for Parents

Breathing out . . . breathing in . . .
giving smiles . . . receiving love . . .

We all give, and we all receive—one way or another—
every single day of our lives.

Have you ever seen the game of "giving" that many

babies play at feeding time? With a twinkle in their eyes, they pop the bottle or spoon out of their mouths and offer it to the grown-up who's feeding them. And what do we grown-ups do in return? Ordinarily, hopefully, we make a "fuss" over the gift, pretending to drink or eat, proclaiming how "deee-licious" it is, and we thank the baby, "Thank you. Thank you."

Being a giver grows out of the experience of having been a receiver— a receiver who has been lovingly given to. The more I've thought about giving, the more obvious it is to me that giving is intimately linked with receiving.

A Young Child's Favorite Gift

One day in the office mail, we received a delightful sur-prise: a package of messages from a preschool class. The teacher of the class had asked the children to tell him what makes them feel happy and what makes them feel sad. The four year olds drew pictures and dictated their thoughts about happy and sad times. Most of the children's messages were about traditional things. But one showed us how much it can mean to a child to be asked to help—especially when the helping is something that's well understood.

"I am happy when I get mom the toilet paper when she calls out from the bathroom!" the child said. It hadn't been that long since that four year old had been helped to be toilet trained. Helping her mother in such a simple way as fetching the needed toilet paper was obviously very meaningful for that little girl.

Most often, it's the adults who are giving help and children who are receiving (or rejecting) our help. As parents, in giving help to a newborn baby, we experience one of the best feelings that any of us can have: that life has meaning because we are needed by someone else. Watching a baby grow with our help tells us other things we like to feel about ourselves: that we are competent and loving.

And of course, the relationship between giving help and love changes—and needs to change—as the relationship between children and their parents grows and changes.

Becoming independent is much more than mastering new skills. One of the most important parts of independence is knowing there are times when you can be helpful by giving things to others.

The Valentine Gifts

Some things we can give; some things we can't, especially when we're very young. We had a letter from a preschool teacher whose group of three year olds delighted in making Valentines for their parents. The teacher decided to add another dimension to the project by suggesting they put the Valentines into envelopes and mail them to their families. That way, she thought, they could also learn about the mail and get an outdoor walk, as well. The children started on their way to the mailbox, proudly carrying their envelopes, but when it came time to put them in the mail slot, they held on to their creations. They refused to let them go! The teacher quickly realized that letting go was just too hard for them, and she revised her plan. They could deliver the envelopes themselves. Later the teacher discovered that some of the children didn't even want to let go of their Valentines to give them to their parents . . . on Valentine's Day itself! Their creations had so much of themselves in them that the Valentines were essentially a part of them, and letting go meant letting go of a part of themselves.

There are certain times in children's lives when they seem to have an extraordinary need to hold on to things. Trying to force them to let go can make them want to hold on even tighter.

Holding on also tends to be a way for some children to react to some other stresses in the family, like the birth of a new baby, starting school, or toilet training. Whatever is causing their uneasiness, children need our patient understanding. Even though it is natural for them to hold on to some things now to help them feel secure, they can still grow up to be people who are generous.

Our Grandson's Gifts

When one of my grandsons was nine years old, his mother took him to a store and told him he could pick out anything he would like to give to his "YeaYea" and "Babba" (that's what he calls my wife and me). His earlier gifts to us were things made in school or chosen with some coaching from his mother and father.

That year, our grandson chose something musical for Joanne (she's a concert pianist), and he chose a small stained glass window ornament (depicting God holding a lamb) for me.

That ornament has been hanging on my window blind ever since, and I see it each morning as I read and pray. I was so touched that Alexander would think that something representing the spiritual life would mean so much to me. Of course, he was right. The gift simply confirmed my belief that, at some point, most children "sense" what their beloved grown-ups consider important.

Growing Towards Being a Charitable Giver

Of course, in earlier years, children aren't able to think of a gift that would fit the interests or needs of people they're close to. It's even more complicated for children to give to people they don't even know, or to some cause halfway around the world—when they aren't even yet familiar with their own city.

I don't think it's helpful to give young children the sense that they are responsible for feeding and clothing all the poor and healing all the ills of the whole world. That's much too heavy a burden for a child. In fact, it could even be frightening for a child to think that he or she might have such responsibility. Children need to know that grown-ups are in charge and that many grown-ups are doing what they can to make this world a better place. We can, however, help children feel they have a part in being a caring neighbor.

Several years ago we heard about an eleven-year-old boy in Philadelphia named Trevor who was watching a local news program on television and saw a story about the plight of the homeless on cold winter nights in the city. When Trevor told his father he didn't think there really were people sleeping on their downtown streets, his father assured him that there were. Touched by the plight of men and women sleeping in the cold, Trevor took one of his own pillows, asked his mother for an extra blanket, and insisted that his parents drive him downtown. Soon they found a man sleeping on the sidewalk, huddled on a steel grate for warmth. Getting out of the car, the boy stooped over the man and kindly offered him the blanket and pillow. Hearing such gratitude in the man's "thank you," Trevor convinced his family to return night after night, distributing blankets, coats, and food—much of which was donated by others who heard about his care for the homeless. What he and his family soon found was that, as they got to know many of the homeless men and women, they themselves came away with a gift—a new respect for the homeless and for their ability to maintain their dignity in spite of their life situations. Trevor went spreading his sense of caring and respect for the homeless to many others in his community as well as in other cities.

The Neighborhood Sweater Drive

For the 30th anniversary of the *Mister Rogers' Neighborhood* program on public television, we invited the local public stations to start their own Neighborhood sweater drive. I knew how tempting it could be to encourage generosity by asking people to help "the needy" or those who are "less fortunate." That kind of thinking divides people into "us" and "them," and doesn't necessarily contribute to a sense of "neighborliness." So we decided to add this message to the people at the stations:

All of us at some time or other need help. Whether we're giving or receiving a sweater, each one of us has something valuable to bring to this world. That's one of the things that connects us as neighbors—in our own way, everyone is a giver and a receiver.

It's far better to say to our children that we are gathering sweaters for people who are cold and don't have the money to buy warm clothing, rather than "for the needy" or "less fortunate."

It may also help to let our children know that people who have money to donate or who have a sweater to give to a clothing drive have other kinds of needs. And those who receive the money or sweater or food have other strengths.

As different as we are from one another, as unique as each one of us is, we are much more the same than we are different. That may be the most essential message of all, as we help our children grow towards being caring, compassionate, and charitable adults.

Charity as a Family Matter

Friends of ours decided to make donations a family matter. Bob and Ann take some of the amount they would regularly donate and divide it among their daughter and son as an allowance. From the allowance, they may spend a third, save one third, and set aside the last third for a donation to a cause. Bob and Ann talk about the work of particular agencies that may interest their children, and on a regular basis, each child decides on a cause to support.

Many of us take care of our donations out of sight of our children. Often our children don't see us taking an action on behalf of others. Just talking about what we do for others can set the foundation for our children's attitudes . . . and we can learn a lot from our children when we hear what kinds of causes are important to them.

One mother was surprised to find out how passionate her children were—and each one about different causes! One son pleaded for the need to give aid to the hungry families in their city, while the other son argued strongly on behalf of third world countries. Their younger sister spoke up for animal shelters. Hopefully, that family will continue to have those discussions over the years. Helping our children consider charitable giving is a process that continues to grow as our children grow.

We also build a caring attitude when we talk about the ways in which we show our care and respect for others—like when we pick up a prescription for a sick neighbor, do volunteer work, give canned food for a homeless shelter, or join in a charity walk-a-thon. Our children hear in our voices what a good feeling it gives us to be a caring neighbor, and that feeling is contagious.

You could also share with your children something about your family's history of giving and receiving. Your children may learn a lot about their heritage by finding out the causes that were important to the past generations of their family—what their ancestors needed to become who they were and what they were able to give to others because of who they became.

My Mother's Christmas Gift

When I was a boy, one of my mother's traditions was knitting sweaters as gifts for our family and close friends. We always knew one of the Christmas boxes would have a hand-knit sweater in it! The older I got, the more I enjoyed receiving mother's sweater gifts, and I always gave her a hug and a kiss whenever I tried on my new one. No wonder sweaters have become a signature part of our "television visits."

But I remember a time when I wasn't such a gracious receiver. I was five years old and very upset when my parents wouldn't buy me a gift I desperately wanted. Even though they helped me understand why I couldn't have that particular gift, I was really disappointed; nevertheless, that early disappointment didn't hurt me. In fact, it helped me to deal with disappointments later in life.

When children aren't being "gracious," they need our ear, our empathy, and our honesty. If we acknowledge our child's right to be disappointed or angry about a present, it can help that child be able to handle those feelings better. A good start may be to say something like, "I know you're disappointed. I realize that it hurts when you don't get what you dreamed of." Maybe you can tell your child about a time you felt like that. (Of course, the specific words we use aren't ever as important as the underlying meaning—that we care about them.)

Over the years I've come to understand a lot about being a gracious receiver. But what a challenge that sometimes can be—for children and for adults. You know, it's much easier to be a giver than a receiver. Givers are in control. They aren't surprised.

Most givers choose their gifts with high hopes that *they* will be appreciated. We long to know that what we have to give is acceptable, that we, too, are acceptable (and loved) as we are. A gift that we give is really like a part of ourselves.

The Soggy Cookie

One way we help children develop an attitude of gratitude is by being gracious receivers when our children do want to give a "gift." Years ago, when I was working with preschoolers at a center, a child lovingly handed me something crumbly in his hand—a soggy cookie. Knowing how important that cookie was to him, I accepted it warmly and ate it. Watching us from the other side of the room, my mentor Dr. Margaret McFarland commented that receiving what a child offers is the greatest thing you can ever do (even though it may not be the most hygienic!).

If a child's gift is not received with gratitude, then it seems as though the gift doesn't have value. More importantly, it seems to the child as though *he* or *she* doesn't have value.

I knew a man who never received gifts with gratitude. Years later, he realized that much of his attitude had to do with his relationship with his father. He sensed that his father never cared for him, never liked him, never acknowledged his worth. How, then, could he acknowledge others?

Kevin's Gift

Receiving a child's gift can sometimes be awkward. I remember a father who wasn't sure what to do about the gift, a pencil holder, his son made for him. Rather crude-looking, made of painted popsicle sticks, decorated with bits of colorful yarn, the holder had a piece of paper pasted on it that said, in a childish scrawl, "I love you, Daddy."

Kevin was only five, and his father didn't feel that he could put this typical piece of five-year-old workmanship on his desk in his formal office—which is exactly where Kevin had said it was meant to go. In fact, it had been hard for that father to know how to respond when he opened this present from his son. What he said was, "What's this? Something you made? Thanks, Kev. It's really nice." And then he just left it where he had opened it.

What we can't always see in a child's gift is all that went into making it. In fact, for young children, the work of making something is usually far more important than the product itself.

Kevin's father found that out by accident the next week, when he happened to meet his son's teacher in a store. The teacher began by telling him how delighted she was finally to meet him because Kevin talked about him all the time. She described how industrious Kevin was.

"Like that pencil holder he made for you," she said. "He worked so long on it—and had such fun with the paint and the paste. I heard him tell the other kids that he was making it for his dad's office." Then she added, "He sure put a lot of himself into that gift."

The pencil holder began to take on a new dimension for Kevin's father—an inner dimension. In fact, it dawned on him that the gift was much more than a place to put pencils. It was a container filled with his son's love. How grateful he was that the teacher had talked with him! He assured his son that the pencil holder was going to have a special place right on his desk at the office. "When I'm at work, I'll be thinking of you and how important you are in my life," he told his son.

The gift and the giver are closely entwined. Being a gracious receiver and showing appreciation for our children's gifts—and other people's gifts—is a very special way to show our love for those givers.

There's an old Quaker saying, "Attitudes are caught, not taught." Children want to be like the people they love, and they learn from seeing that their favorite adults care about their neighbors—even those whom they don't know—and are gracious about giving and receiving even the simplest of gifts.

May you and your family find unexpected joys in your own giving—and receiving—all through your lives.

Fred Rogers

Mister Rogers' Message for Children

Right from the time when you were born, you needed someone to give you food and fresh diapers, a place to sleep, and most of all—love. Hopefully, the people in your family gave all that to you.

Even as a baby, you gave things to them,

too, things like smiles and the good feeling of taking good care of you, and most of all— love. You see, even as a baby, you already knew a lot about giving and receiving.

Of course, as you grew, you started to be able to do some things for yourself, like feed yourself and get dressed yourself. But you still needed a family to buy and fix the food for you, to make sure you had a place to sleep, and to give you love. Your gifts to them grew, too. You could give hugs and make all kinds of sounds, and when you learned to talk, you could tell your family what you were thinking and feeling. That's an extra special gift because it comes right from your heart, and it helps people get to know the special person that you are.

So over the years you have found many ways to say, "I love you," like saying it out loud, drawing pictures for someone, writing a note, eating something special someone made just for you, cleaning up a room when someone asks you to do it. Those are a few of your special gifts.

You also know how good it feels when someone gives you help when you need something, like a towel when you get out of a bathtub, a sweater on a cold day, some food when you're hungry, or some water when you're thirsty, or a hug when you're feeling sad.

And you know how good it feels when you, yourself, can be a "helper." You have many ways to help people, like when you bring something they've asked for, sing a song that makes a baby brother or sister stop crying, put the napkins on the table for dinner, bring a tissue when someone has a cold, or put your arm around a friend who is sad.

We can even give help to and receive help from people we don't know. On our television program, I sing "Won't you be my neighbor?" Neighbors are people who care about and help each other. Sometimes they live in the same real neighborhood. But they can also be "neighbors" even if they live far away. They might even live in a different country, where people talk differently or wear different clothes, or eat different foods, but they can still be our "neighbors." They can still be people we care about, just because they're human beings.

Every person in this world started out as a baby needing food and diapers and a place to sleep and most of all—love. In fact, every person started out just like you; so you see, we can all be givers and we can all be receivers. The best givers and the best receivers are people who really care about their neighbors, just as they care about themselves.

Mister Rogers

Folktales and Fables

About Sharing These Stories with Children

Has anyone ever said to you, "Let me tell you a story about . . . ?" Do you remember perking up your ears? If so, do you remember waiting with anticipation for what might come next? Once you heard it, you might have even wanted to pass that story on to someone else. Stories can be like magnets. They attract us. And they tend to stick with us for a long, long time. You may still remember stories you heard when you were a little child.

It's no wonder, then, that from the beginning of time, adults used stories as a way of passing on their treasured morals, values, and attitudes to their children. Human beings are storytellers. In fact, in some ways, the story of any one of us is the story of us all.

Since stories are often told to us by people whom we love and are told in loving ways, they're like gifts being given to us. It's only natural that such stories would stay with us—in our minds and in our hearts.

To help you and your children begin to talk about such things as giving and receiving, we have included in this book some folktales and fables from around the world. Since stories were first passed on orally, from generation to generation, each storyteller added his or her own personal twist to it. You are invited to do the same. Tell the story in your own words or read it in your own "voice." No matter what, you'll be adding your own personality to it. Just the fact that it's coming from you makes the story a unique gift for your child.

Maybe these folktales and fables will inspire you to look for other such tales to share with your children. Maybe some of your relatives remember stories told to them in their childhood. Tales that come from your family's own culture and background can take on even more meaning.

It's certainly not necessary to read all the stories in this section in one sitting. You might want to start with one or two that are your favorites. The ones you feel comfortable with are more likely to be remembered by your child. Your emotional investment in whatever you read or say is what makes it truly "magnetic."

Hopefully you'll enjoy the stories . . . and the sharing . . . just as much as your child does.

The Brothers

Some folktales about brothers are stories of rivalry and jealousy. But there are also tales, like this one, of warm and strong bonds between two brothers and obligations to take care of one another. This Hebrew legend is about a puzzling mystery.

Two brothers inherited equal parts of their father's fields. They were both successful farmers; they were both kind and caring towards each other.

As the years went by, the older brother married. He and his wife had three sons. The younger brother remained single.

For a long time both brothers did well on their farms; however, one year there was no rain. Most of the crops withered in the fields. There was little wheat that could be harvested.

The older brother said to his wife and sons, "I am worried about my brother. He is all alone. He has no wife or children to care for him. Even though we harvested little this year on our farm, I want to share some of what we have with my brother. If I offer some of our food, he will probably refuse it. So I'll just put it in his barn." In the middle of the night, he piled some of his wheat into a cart and quietly left it in his brother's barn.

That same night, the younger brother awoke. He thought about how many mouths his brother had to feed. And he decided to share what little he had with him and his family. "Surely he'll kindly refuse my wheat if I offer it." So in the middle of the night, he secretly carted some of his wheat to his brother's barn.

The next morning, when the older brother went out to his barn, he couldn't believe his eyes! How could it be that he gave some of his wheat to his brother, but his pile of wheat was as high as the day before?

When the younger brother went out to his barn that same morning, he couldn't believe his eyes! How could it be that he gave some of his wheat to his brother, but his pile of wheat was as high as the day before? What a mystery!

Again the next night, each brother went out to share some of his wheat with the other one. And again, the next morning, each brother found in the barn the same amount of wheat as the day before!

The older brother talked about this mystery with his wife and sons, and they decided to go along with him that night. Maybe they could help him figure it out.

The whole family pitched in, and soon they had stacked a high pile of wheat in their cart. Could it be that their father had just misjudged how much he had delivered? The puzzled family started on their way.

The younger brother, also puzzled, started on his way with his cart. It so happened that night that both brothers chose to cart their wheat at the same time. And lo and behold! They met in the middle of the fields, each with wheat for the other! How they all laughed and hugged, when they realized what was behind the mystery—their own kindness for each other!

The Countess and the Miracle

This story comes from Northern Italy at a time when there were royal palaces and castles. There were also many poor people in the land, so being charitable was especially important. Some of the noblemen were kind and generous to the poor, but some were not. This story is about how one nobleman learned to be charitable.

There once was a countess who was as kind-hearted as she was beautiful. Her greatest pleasure in life was helping the poor. But her husband was as greedy as she was generous. He forbade his wife to take their money or food to give away to others—even though they had so much. Just to make sure, he put a heavy lock on the storage room where they kept their food. "If we give it away, we'll be poor ourselves," he told his wife.

The Countess pleaded with her husband to share some of their food with the poor. But he refused. She prayed for a miracle that might change her hard-hearted husband's ways.

One day, she happened to be walking by the storage room and accidentally brushed up against the lock. Miraculously, the door opened. She quickly gathered up in her apron some loaves of bread, fruit, and cheese to give to the poor, and another miracle happened! Even though she took food from the shelves, more food appeared in its place.

Day after day, she made her trip to the poor with her apron full of bread, fruit, and cheese.

Her husband soon became suspicious. He noticed that she was no longer sad and that the poor were no longer starving. Hiding in the shadows, he followed her and watched her go into the storage room. Out she came with a bulging apron.

"Show me what you have there," he demanded of her.

"Why . . . it's just something sweet and makes people happy . . . It's . . . it's . . . just roses," she answered.

When her husband reached out, asking for one, even she was surprised to see she was indeed carrying an apron full of yellow roses. Astonished, her husband took one of the roses and attached it to the brim of his hat. He walked off, proud of his lovely flower decoration.

As soon as he left, the Countess felt the weight grow heavier in her apron. Once again, she was carrying loaves of bread. She said a prayer of thanks to the Lord and went off smiling to help feed the poor.

Meanwhile, her husband took a walk over to the courtyard where workmen were repairing some broken stones. He was holding his head high, feeling rather regal with his flower in his hat.

So why were the workmen laughing at him? What were they pointing at with ridicule?

"What are you laughing at?"

They pointed to his hat and laughed all the more.

"What's wrong with my hat?" he asked them. And just to see for himself, he took off his hat. And then he saw that what he thought had been a yellow rose was instead—a loaf of bread!

"So that's what my wife had in her apron," he thought to himself—and then he realized that, all along, the Lord in Heaven must have wanted them to give food to the poor.

From that day on, as if by some miracle, his heart was changed! He became just as charitable and loved as his wife, the kindly Countess.

The Lion and the Mouse

Aesop's fables are short stories with strong and clear morals. In most tales, animals are given human characteristics, so that children can take the messages into their everyday lives. This is a story about how we can all help each other, whether we're big or small.

There was once a sleepy lion who found the perfect spot for a nap in the forest. He lay down and soon fell fast asleep. While he was sleeping, a tiny mouse came by. The mouse thought he had come to a big rock. So he climbed up. But it wasn't a big rock at all. It was the face of the big lion!

The lion felt something tickling his face, woke up with a start, and grabbed the mouse with his paw. He was about to crush the mouse, when he heard a tiny voice begging him to let go.

"If you let me go now," said the tiny mouse, "I will help you some day."

"Silly mouse," said the lion. "How can *you* ever help me! I'm big and mighty. You're small. What can you do?" The lion laughed and laughed and laughed—and let him go.

A while later, some hunters came into the forest. They set a trap for the lion. It was a great big net, and the mighty lion got caught in it and couldn't get out.

Along came the tiny mouse. When he saw that the lion was trapped in the net, he realized he could indeed be of real help, so he began doing what comes naturally to mice—he started using his sharp teeth! He gnawed, and he gnawed, and he gnawed. Soon, he had made a hole big enough for the lion to escape.

"Oh, thank you, little mouse," said the big lion. "I now know for sure that even a little mouse can do mighty important things."

The Gift of the Farmer

This story is a variation of a Bulgarian folktale about the great value of a gift that comes from the heart. When someone offers something precious to him or her, something from the heart, that gift has enormous value. The person who chooses to receive the gift of the heart is greatly rewarded in the end.

There once was a family of three brothers. When the boys grew old enough to go out on their own, they went out to seek their fortunes. But they decided to go their separate ways. They planned to meet in three years to see how each of them had done.

The eldest brother became a baker. His cakes, breads, and pastries were so delicious that his bakery was always full of customers. At the end of the three years, he had a bagful of gold coins.

The next brother opened an inn where travelers could eat and sleep. His meals were so tasty and his beds so comfortable that his inn was always filled with travelers. At the end of three years, he, too, had a bagful of gold coins.

The youngest brother met up with a farmer who needed help planting and harvesting vegetables. This brother agreed to work for the farmer for three years. He was a hard worker, and his carrots and beans and potatoes grew so well that the farmer received many gold coins from selling the vegetables at the market place. The old farmer took very good care of this brother, making sure he had good meals and a comfortable place to live.

At the end of three years, the youngest brother thanked the farmer for his kindness and asked for his payment for all the work that he had done.

The farmer brought out two bags. One was full of gold coins. He said, "You earned this gold because of all the hard work that you did to make this farm so successful. But, this gold is just money. And money can bring people many problems. You may want to choose what's in this other bag instead. It is a gift from my heart."

The farmer opened the smaller bag. He reached in and pulled out three walnuts. These nuts were given to me by my own father before he died years ago. I've kept them close to me ever since. They're my most precious possession because they always remind me of my father. You have been like a son to me, and these walnuts are a gift from my heart."

It didn't take the youngest brother long to make his decision. He chose the three walnuts instead of the gold coins. He thanked the farmer and set out to meet his older brothers.

At their meeting place, the eldest brother proudly brought out his bagful of gold coins. The next brother just as proudly brought out his bag with just as many gold coins. After congratulating each other, they turned to the youngest brother.

"And what have you to show for your work these three years?" they asked him.

The youngest brother showed them the three ordinary looking walnuts. The other brothers laughed out loud.

"But they were a gift from the farmer's heart," he said. "He offered me a bagful of gold coins, but these walnuts were far more precious than gold to him. Since he was like a father to me, these walnuts are more precious than gold to me."

"That's ridiculous," the older brothers said, "You must go back and ask the farmer for the gold."

Wondering if they may have been right, the youngest brother started back to find the old farmer. Along the way, he became hungry and thought of the walnuts. They wouldn't be very filling, but they could help a bit. As he cracked the first walnut open, something wondrous happened! The nut grew and grew and grew. Finally, out of it stepped a sturdy horse with a shiny new plow and a cart full of seeds for vegetables and fruit trees.

Wide-eyed, the brother wondered what might be in the other walnuts. He started to crack the second one, and something even more wondrous happened. It grew and grew and grew—and out of it rolled a rack of magnificent clothing, a warm coat, and shiny new boots.

Excited about what he might find inside the third walnut, he started to crack it. It grew and grew and grew. Out of it came a lovely woman who spoke caringly to him.

Wearing his fine new clothes, he invited the lovely woman to join him on his new horse. Together they rode down the road to the farm, with the cart full of things to plant. The old farmer greeted him with great surprise.

When he heard the story, he said, "I always knew the walnuts were precious, but I had no idea why. They were just a gift from the heart."

Soon there were wedding plans for the brother and the lovely woman. When his brothers arrived for the wedding, they were amazed. Their youngest brother had taught them not to put such high value on gold, for one could easily miss the wondrous things that come from receiving a gift from the heart.

The Gold in the Ground

From Kazakh, on the Steppes of central Asia, comes this tale about how unselfishness and good-heartedness can reap rich rewards in the long run. Just think about how many kind people all through this story made caring decisions that contributed to the happy ending.

There once were two friends, a farmer and a shepherd. They both were poor, but they worked hard and cared about each other. When a disease killed all of the shepherd's sheep, his friend the farmer gave him some land for him to begin farming.

"As my friend, you have half my heart. Please take half my land."

So it was because of the kindness of his friend that the shepherd began to plow his half of the land. What should he find there, as he dug in the field? A pot of gold!

He took the pot of gold to the farmer. "It came from the field that you gave me. The gold is yours."

"Oh, no," said the farmer, "You did the work of digging it out of the ground. You found it. The gold is yours."

The two friends argued a while, but they had an idea. One had a daughter and the other had a son who had great affection for each other. They hoped to marry each other, but had no money. Now the fathers had a way to help them both. They could give the pot of gold to their children.

After the wedding, though, the young couple came to their fathers to return the gold. "It isn't right for us to keep this. We should not have the benefit of money that really belongs to our fathers." And no talking could convince them otherwise.

Now what could the fathers do! Again they argued, each wanting the other to have the gold. They came up with a new plan. They would ask advice from the man who was known to be the wisest in the land.

Traveling with the gold, they came to the hut of the wise man and found him there with four young students. When the wise man heard their story, he asked his students what they would suggest.

The first student said, "I would give the gold to the leader of our land, the khan, as he owns all the treasures found in our land. It should be his."

The wise man shook his head. That answer

did not make him happy.

The second student said, "I would give the gold to the farmers because the court would say that it is theirs."

The wise man frowned, not happy with this answer either.

The third student said, "I would put the gold back into the ground where I found it since no one will accept it."

The wise man held his head in his hands, not pleased with this answer either.

The last student said, "I would use the gold to buy seeds and plant those seeds in the poorest section of our country, so that those who are poor and hungry will have food to eat."

Hearing that answer, the wise man hugged the fourth student for his caring advice.

"That's what should be done with the pot of gold," he said. "And you will be blessed for thinking of those who are hungry and for finding a way to help them."

The young student set off with the pot of gold to buy the seeds for grain, fruits, and vegetables. On his way to the marketplace, he heard the chiming of many caravan bells and loud screeching noises. On the backs of camels, he saw cages and cages of trapped birds crying for their freedom. Overcome by his feelings for the birds, the young man approached the caravan leader. "Here is a pot full of gold. That should pay for all those birds. Let them free."

The caravan leader thought the young man was joking, but when he saw all the gold, he grabbed it and ordered the birds to be set free. With a great flapping of their wings, the birds flew off out of their cages and into the sky.

As he walked along, the student felt good about freeing the birds. As he watched the birds fly, he was filled with great joy. But, all of a sudden, his heart sank. He started to doubt the wisdom of what he had done. How could he have just given the money to the caravan leader? It wasn't his money. And now the poor in the land would remain hungry! Tired and discouraged, the student sat down under the shelter of a tree and fell asleep.

Out of nowhere came a magnificent bird with a lovely voice, singing to the young man, "You have done such a kind deed in freeing us. We can't get your gold back, but we can help in other ways. Just wait and see."

When the young man opened his eyes, he saw an astonishing sight. In the fields around him were hundreds of birds, pecking away at the ground, dropping seeds into the holes they dug! And magically, the seedlings turned into shoots and into plants and trees, full of fruits and vegetables. There was no finer farm in all the land!

He ran back to the wise man, ecstatic about what he had seen. Soon all throughout the land, the poor and hungry heard about this magnificent farm that was for just them.

They walked through the magic garden, sharing with each other the abundant food growing there.

The farmer and the shepherd smiled to each other. With their own eyes, they saw what good came from their pot of gold—and kindness and generosity, too.

How the Chipmunk Got Its Stripes

American Indian legends are sacred stories. They tell of the love of the earth, the interdependence of all living things, and respect for nature. Here is a story with all three messages.

All through the winter, the bear did what all bears do in the winter—he slept. He had a long, long sleep in the cold, cold winter.

When spring came, the sun began to shine, warming up the world. The snow melted. The river water began to run. Now it was time for the bear to wake up. He stretched one paw and then another. He climbed out of the cave that had been his home all through the winter.

What do you suppose he wanted first of all? Something to eat!

"I'm really hungry," said the big bear. "I wonder what there is to eat?"

"Maybe some berries," he said to himself. And he lumbered down to the berry patch. But no berries were on the branches yet. It was too soon for a meal of berries.

So the bear went on, looking for something to satisfy his big hunger.

He walked on down to the river. But there were only twigs and leaves floating in the river. So he went on, still looking for something . . . anything . . . good to eat.

"Maybe some grubs," he said to himself. And he lumbered over and clawed at the ground under a rotten tree stump. But there were no grubs there.

Now the bear was really hungry . . . and really frustrated. He put his nose between his big paws, and he began to cry with a loud wail. Then he started to stomp around in a hungry rage.

He stomped so hard that it shook the ground. Under the tree stump was a tiny chipmunk who couldn't imagine what was making such a racket. He came scampering out of his home in the ground and saw the big bear. "What's wrong?" he asked.

The bear looked down at the chipmunk, and he said, "I'm really hungry!"

"Oh," said the chipmunk, "I can help with that! I have all kinds of nuts and berries in my home. Before winter sets in, I store them away so I have something to eat in the spring-time. I've got plenty."

He ran down his hole into his home and came back carrying in his cheeks some berries that had dried over the winter and some nuts he had gathered from the trees. He dropped the nuts and berries beside the giant paws of the bear and said, "Here, have some. I'm glad to share them with you."

Gratefully, the bear began to eat. But he was a big bear. And he was very hungry. The chipmunk was tiny and couldn't carry many nuts and berries at a time. So he had to make lots of trips from his home to the bear until the bear had enough to eat.

"Well, little chipmunk," said the bear. "You may be a tiny animal, but you have a very big heart. You have been so kind to me." And the bear reached out with his giant paw and gently stroked the back of the tiny chipmunk. With the five claws on his paw, he left five long marks from the front to the back of the chipmunk.

"Now you have a mark of your kindness," said the bear to the chipmunk. "Whenever people see your stripes, they will think of your kindness."

So whenever you see a chipmunk, you, too, can remember that gifts of kindness come from a very big heart.

The Lesson of the Birds

The Agikuyu tribe settled in Kenya, a lush part of Southern Africa in the sixteenth century. The farmland was rich there, but required a great deal of work. This story shows how important it was for the farmers to give and receive help from each other. Mutual helping was one of their greatest resources.

There once was a hard-working old man who had the most successful farm in all the countryside. After he died, his only son took over the farm.

The son knew there had been a huge harvest from his father's fields. There was much food stored away.

"Surely," he thought, "I won't have to work as hard as my father. In fact, I won't have to work at all! I can just lay around all day and still have plenty to eat." Silently, he thanked his father for his good fortune.

Day after day, month after month, the son slept in the sun. When he got too hot, he moved to the shade of a tree. Soon everything on the farm started to spoil. Because no one took care of the fields, they became too dry when there was no rain and too muddy when there was too much rain. Nothing was planted. Nothing was growing.

The understanding of all who lived in this land was that everyone helped each other. The farms were too much work for just one family. And everyone gave a hand to neighbors on nearby farms. But no one helped the son. No one wanted to give a hand to a lazy man who helped no one else!

One hot and sunny afternoon, the son was sleeping as usual. All of a sudden, flapping noises awakened him, and he was surprised to see a flock of "weaver birds" flapping their wings and busily going hither and thither gathering little bits of things in their beaks.

He realized it was nesting time, and he saw how each bird did its part, collecting twigs to build nests. They were all helping each other. At the end of the day, he was amazed to see that with all their hard work and cooperation, the tiny birds had made the frames of many sturdy nests.

The next day, he saw the birds returning, this time to help each other weave bits of grasses into their nests so their families would have soft, cozy places to live. And just in time! By evening there was a big rainstorm, but the bird families were able to find shelter in the nests they had made.

Day after day, the birds continued to work together, until they had built a colony of nests—enough for the whole flock. And day after day, the son marveled at how much the birds had accomplished by helping each other. Then he thought about how little he was accomplishing with his two powerful hands.

The next day, he awoke early, picked up one of his hoes, and went to a neighbor's field. With his hands, he pulled and tugged at the weeds and grasses. Then he picked up his hoe and began working the soil. Soon other neighboring farmers joined in, and he was friendly to them. At the end of the day, he was tired but happy—as happy as a "weaver bird."

No one asked for his help, but each day he went to a neighboring farm to give a hand. He asked for nothing in return.

One morning he awoke to hear chattering coming from his own farm, which had become terribly overgrown with weeds and brambles. In his fields, his neighbors were cheerfully working hard to clear the ground. He came right out to join them, and together they made the field ready for planting.

After a while, fruits and vegetables were growing again on his farmland. When harvest time came, he and his neighbors helped each other with the crops. He knew whom to thank for his good fortune—his father who gave him the land, the neighbors who helped him farm the land, and the "weaver birds" who had taught him that hard work, unselfishness, and cooperation bring the greatest rewards of all.

Only Three Questions

Asian tales often have mythical characters, like dragons and serpents who have great magical powers. In this Chinese folktale, there is a serpent who has such power, but there's even greater power that comes from kindness.

There was a man in China who had much money. He had been born into a family of great fortune, and he was given a name that meant "million." In those days, names were thought to have great power, and when he came of age, indeed this man did have a million pieces of gold. With his family background and his name, he lived his life as though he would always have a "million."

Million was a kindly man. Instead of using his riches for himself, he shared his wealth with people who were hungry and poor. Out of the goodness of his heart, he gave food or shelter to all those who asked.

After many years of such generosity, he had little money left. His clothes became ragged. Without money to buy coal for his fireplace, he was cold. And he was hungry. Even then, he gave what little he had to those who needed it.

One day, as he was sharing half of his bowl of rice with someone hungrier than he, Million asked himself, "How is it that I am poor and no longer able to help others? I have not been selfish. I come from a family of fortune and have done only kindly things for others. Why haven't I been rewarded with more money to use for helping those who are poor or hungry?"

He knew a place he could go for the answer to his question.

Over the years people have told him about Kuan-yin, the merciful, wise serpent goddess who knew the past and the future. And she allowed each person who visited her to ask three questions. With a hopeful heart, Million started on his long journey to Kuan-yin's home in the South Sea.

On his way, he came upon a river that he needed to cross. But the river was wide, and it was flowing so fast that Million feared for his life. He cried out, "How will I get to Kuan-yin to ask my question!" From high above the tree tops, a huge snake overheard him and called out, "So you're going to the South Sea? Would you please ask Kuan-yin a question for me?"

Million promised to help. Adding the snake's question to his own would not be a problem.

The grateful snake said, "Please ask her why I am not a magnificent dragon yet, even though I have been unselfish and disciplined for more than a thousand years."

Million said he would ask the question for the snake. But how could he get to the goddess, when the raging river stopped him from continuing on his way? "Water is no problem for me," said the snake. "And since you agree to take my question to Kuan-yin, just jump on my back, and I'll carry you across."

Together they crossed the river safely. Million thanked the snake and continued towards the South Sea. Soon he became hungry, and he stopped for some food at an inn. As he waited for his bowl of rice, he told the innkeeper about his travels.

"Oh, sir," said the innkeeper. "Since you're

going to Kuan-yin, would you please ask her a question for me? I have a beautiful daughter. She is twenty years old, and she is caring and sweet. But she has never spoken a word— ever. Would you please ask the goddess how we can help her speak?"

Touched by the innkeeper's plea, Million promised to help. Adding the innkeeper's question would not be a problem. Now he had his three questions to ask—his own, the snake's, and the innkeeper's.

Million left the village and traveled toward the South Sea through the rest of the day. When nighttime came, he needed a place to sleep. Seeing no inns nearby, he went up to the largest house in the village and asked for lodging. The owner, a rich man, answered the door and graciously took him in, offering a meal and a bed. When he heard about the reason for the journey, the rich man begged for help, too.

"For many years, I have taken good care of my garden," he said. "But nothing here blooms. Since you're going to the South Sea, would you please ask Kuan-yin why I have no fruit or flowers in my garden?"

Million thought, "Even though I already have three questions, how can I refuse, after such kindness has been given to me?" So he promised he would ask.

So now he had four questions! If he left out his own, his trip would be for nothing. If he left out one of the others', he would be breaking his promise. But he continued on his way, being sure that some good would come from such a journey. And even *some* good would be better for the world.

Finally, Million arrived at the South Sea and was called in to meet with Kuan-yin. His first question was for the snake who wanted to know, "How can I become a magnificent dragon?" The serpent goddess answered,

"There are seven bright pearls on his head. If he removes six of them, he will become a dragon."

Million's second question was for the innkeeper. "How can the innkeeper's daughter become able to speak?" The serpent goddess answered, "She will be able to speak when she sees the man who will be her husband."

Million hesitated for a moment, but knew in his heart what he had to ask. His third question would not be for himself, but for the rich man. "How can the rich man's garden begin to bloom and bear fruit?" The serpent goddess answered, "Buried in his garden are seven large jars of silver and gold. If he gives away half his treasure, his garden will be full of flowers and fruit." Then the serpent goddess said, "You have asked three questions, and I noticed that they are all for others. You are a kind-hearted man. Do not think that your generosity went unnoticed." And with those words, Kuan-yin disappeared.

Million started the long journey back to his own village, somewhat discouraged about not being able to ask his own question, but grateful for the serpent's caring words.

First he came to the rich man's home and told him Kuan-yin's answer to his question. Immediately, the rich man began digging in the garden and found the jars of silver and gold. He gave half of the treasure to Million, knowing that soon his garden would become full of beautiful flowers and delicious fruit.

Next Million came to the inn. A sweet voice called out to him through a window of the inn. It was the innkeeper's daughter, asking about the answer to her father's question! Hearing her voice, the innkeeper was astounded. He could see the caring way his daughter and Million looked at each other. Just as Kuan-yin predicted—here was the man she would marry! With great joy, the innkeeper's daughter and Million were married.

Now traveling home with his new wife, Million approached the flowing river where the snake sat in the grass waiting for him. He told the snake about Kuan-yin's answer to his question. In gratitude, the snake removed six of his bright pearls and gave them to the newlyweds. As he did so, the snake turned into a magnificent dragon who immediately helped them cross the river in grand style.

And so it was that this good and generous man, through his own kindness and care for others, was once more worth a million pieces of gold, with enough money for his family and for anyone who came to him in need.

Using the Giving Box

Using the Giving Box can give you an opportunity to think about and talk about how everyone in your family is a giver and a receiver—a helper and someone in need of help. Just recognizing the giving and receiving can elevate those moments that are a part of everyday life—and help everyone to be a real part of the giving and receiving that's already happening in your family.

Our message to parents at the beginning of this book may

help you find your own ways to start conversations about giving and receiving. In addition, you may want to start by asking your child what the word "helping" means, or how he or she helps others and is helped by others. You could also talk about the many ways you and your family show love to each other. In our television program, we often sing "There Are Many Ways to Say I Love You." There's the eating way and the cooking way. Even cleaning up a room can say "I love you."

Many families have a history of giving and receiving help. If you know of them, let your children know some ways your ancestors have given, served, or been helped. What charities were important in their lives? What traditions of helping or being helped, giving or receiving charity, have been important in your life?

Putting Money in the Box

If you put the Giving Box in a place where you and the children can see it—like on a kitchen counter or on a table in the living room, it can become an integral part of your home. If you see it every day and use it regularly, you and your children are more likely to think about what the box represents and be reminded of being charitable.

You and your child might want to develop your own family rituals for putting money in the box. Children love rituals. Rituals are predictable and regular. Rituals become traditions, and they make memories, as well.

Find a regular time that's best for your family to put money in the box—at the end of the day or at the end of the week or in the morning of a holiday. Then putting money in the box becomes a ritual—something that children come to expect and participate in on a regular basis.

Your children may want to put money in the box at other times, like when someone is thankful for something good that's happened, or when someone has done something to help them, or when someone has returned from a trip.

There are a number of ways to involve your child in putting the money in the box. Maybe you want to give your child some coins to put into the box. Children may even like the sound of the coin going into the box. If you give your child an allowance, you may want to suggest putting a part of it in the box. If children don't want to "let go" of the money to put it in the box, that's okay, too. If they aren't ready for that yet, it doesn't mean that they're selfish. "Holding on" may be important to your child at a particular time. Maybe your child would like to put his or her hand on yours while you're dropping the money into the box. And it may help you to remember that it takes a while for children to develop a charitable perspective. But you're doing the important work of building that foundation when your child sees—right there at home—that being charitable is important to you.

When the Box Is Full

Every year, billions of dollars are donated to charity. Your family can feel proud to continue that philanthropic tradition.

Maybe you already know of some charitable causes that may be of interest to your family or to your child. Some families decide beforehand where to donate the money. Others wait until afterwards when the box is full. You may want to involve your child in the decision about where the money goes and talk about how those causes help people. Participating in the decision can help your child feel an important part of the ways your family is charitable. If you have several children, you may want to divide the money from the box among your children and let each make a separate donation.

It may be easier for your child to relate to a charitable cause if it's a local one. You may want to contact someone at a local church, synagogue, mosque, or United Way agency. That person can give you names of agencies that aid children, families, or causes that could be of interest to your family.

If you hear, in the news or through your community, about a local family in need because of a house fire or other hard times, you may want to suggest donating all or some of the money from the box to that family.

If you send the money to a charity, encourage your child to write (or help you write) a note or draw a picture to send along with the donation.

Some agencies or families receiving donations write thank-you notes to donors. If you receive a note like that, be sure to show it to your child and read it aloud. You can all rejoice in knowing that your donation has really helped your "neighbors."

The Tzedaka Box

Tzedaka, *the Jewish word for charity, comes from the Hebrew word* tzedek *which means "a righteous person." According to Jewish law, a person is obligated to be generous. A tzedaka box is a tin box in the home for collecting coins to donate to a particular charity. Families generally put money in the tzedaka box to ask forgiveness from God or to express thanks to God.*

The Mite Box

Some churches give their congregants a mite box or a "thankfulness" box to take home to remind them to be involved with mission. When the box is full, it is emptied into a larger box at the church, then sent to help a particular cause.

The mite box is often linked to the story of the widow's mite, in which Jesus saw some rich people putting their gifts into the treasury. He also saw a poor widow putting in two copper coins. Jesus said that the widow put in more than all the others because she was very poor and gave everything she had. (Luke 21:1–4)

Beyond the Box

Giving has to do with far more than money. After all, children have little or no money of their own. But they certainly have the capacity to be "givers" in other ways. And because children often need so much help—even with everyday things, they might think that children are the only ones who do. But you can let them know that everyone in this world needs some kind of help . . . and that some people need more help than others.

Encouraging children to be helpful is one of the best ways to help them develop a charitable attitude, and that's an attitude that hopefully will grow all through their lives.

Some Family Activities

Making coupons can be a fun way for your child to offer help to family members. If you cut some pieces of paper in the shape of a coupon, your child can write or draw on them some ideas of helpful things to give, like "a hug," "some quiet time on a Saturday morning," "help with a household chore," "reading a book to a younger brother or sister." Coupons are like a promise to help at some future time, and they can be meaningful gifts to people in the family.

Plan to help in a "soup kitchen" to serve a Thanksgiving or Christmas Day meal. When you do that as a family, you're serving together, and your children can see how much your family's help is appreciated by others.

If you volunteer for a charitable organization, like delivering "meals on wheels," or visiting a nursing home, invite your child to join you, if it's allowed. Children can be such a welcome sight to people who are housebound, and the children can really feel appreciated when they see how much joy they bring to others.

You might want to suggest that your child's youth group, Sunday school class, or Scout troop focus on a particular charity, learn about what the needs are, and make crafts to sell or raise money in other ways to donate to that cause. You may want to search the Internet to find out more about charities or causes that are interesting to children.

When it comes time to give a gift for a birthday or anniversary or other special occasion, you could encourage your child to offer something he or she has created. Some children we know have had great fun making up and performing a "skit" or a poem or singing their own words to a familiar song to honor a family member. Others have given pictures they have made. Gifts that come from our homespun talents and our love can be even more memorable and priceless than any present that can be bought.

Making thank-you notes is a simple way to encourage your child to be gracious. Children might feel more inclined to write thank-you notes when they've designed the cards themselves.

Look for opportunities to say "thank you" to your child, when your child has done something kind or caring for you or for someone else. If children hear "thank you" at home, they're more likely to say it to others.

One way to show your appreciation for a picture or other gift your child has made for you is to display it on a kitchen wall or under a magnet on the refrigerator or at the office.

If you know a family that has a child with a disability, encourage your child to visit and be a friendly "neighbor" to that child—play with or read to that child. The gift of our time and attention is one of the best gifts of all.

If you know a family that is having some financial or medical difficulties, you might invite them for a meal and maybe play some board games or work on a puzzle together.

Is there an elderly neighbor who could benefit from a visit from your family? So many lonely people brighten up and are especially grateful for a chat or visit with a child. Maybe your child could also volunteer to help that person by taking out the garbage, walking the dog, cutting the lawn, or shoveling the walkway.

If there are recent immigrants in your area, you might consider "adopting" a family through an agency, by reaching out to them, treating them to a meal, and helping them understand about things that are everyday experiences for American families—going to the library or to a playground or to a shopping mall. Asking them to teach you about their country's customs and helping you to learn words from their native language will not only help you but will also show that your family respects what their family has to give.

When you're reading newspapers or magazines, look for articles that have to do with someone who needs food or shelter, or someone who does some special kindness. If you bring those clippings to read and talk about at the dinner table, you're opening your child's eyes to lots of different ways in which people contribute to making this a better world.

When I was a boy and would hear about something upsetting or scary in the news, I would ask my parents or my grandparents about it. And they would usually tell me how they felt about it. In fact, my mother would try to find out who was helping the person who got hurt. "Always

look for the helpers," she'd tell us. "You'll always find some-
body who's trying to help." So even today, when I read the
newspaper or magazines or see the news on television, I look
for the people who are doing their best to help . . . not in
sensational ways but in the little genuine ways that nourish
neighbors' lives.

"No act of kindness, no matter
how small, is ever wasted."

(Aesop)

"Friendship is one of the greatest gifts
a human being can receive."

(Henri J.M. Nouwen)

"Love thy neighbor as thyself."

(Leviticus 19:18; Matthew 19:19)

"The best way to find yourself is to lose
yourself in the service of others."

(Gandhi)

Special Thanks

My parents and grandparents were generous givers and gracious receivers. They made charity and service central in our family by their example and by letting us know in many ways how much that was valued by them.

I was also very fortunate to have two mentors who were not only generous in their teaching, but generous in their living. I learned from them far more than the "information" they were teaching. Dr. Margaret B. McFarland, our long-term psychological consultant for our Neighborhood programs, helped me to understand the roots of giving and receiving, as well as the important role of adults in the process of developing generosity and gratitude. And Dr. William Orr, one of my beloved professors at the Pittsburgh Theological Seminary, gave me and all of his students a deep spiritual sense of charity, and a very real sense of it. He would often come to teach our class at the seminary after being out on a wintry day, walking in without a coat because he had given his to someone along the way who needed it.

Our long-term staff member, Hedda Bluestone Sharapan,

took on the work of research and development for this book with passion and dedication. She brought to this project, as she does to all her work, her deep understanding of children from her child development background, and her years of service with us, and her own family heritage. Another long-time staff member, Cathy Cohen Droz, has worked closely with every word in the manuscript and every part of the design. Grateful thanks to both of them; they embody generosity. Thanks, too, to Vijay Palaparty, Colette Sharp, and Lynne Farbotnik, our interns who graciously helped us in many different ways.

Extra thanks to our good friend Dr. Margaret Mary Kimmel of the University of Pittsburgh School of Library and Information Sciences, who has always willingly and enthusiastically consulted with us over the years about children's literature. Her support and her vast knowledge of folktales were invaluable. We are grateful to Dr. Kimmel's former student, Liza Purdy. Under Dr. Kimmel's guidance and with her own library skills, Liza spent hours sifting through indices and hundreds of tales researching stories for this book. We also appreciate the extra help of Dr. Kimmel's colleagues, Elizabeth Mahoney and Kathy Maron-Woods.

Special thanks to our friends at Running Press and especially to our editor, Patricia Smith, for her warm and continuing encouragement.

And, of course, our deep gratitude for all the support that always comes from everyone on the staff of our little company, Family Communications, Inc. It's our day-to-day giving and receiving that continually nourishes us all in everything that we do.

About the Author

Fred McFeely Rogers was born in 1928 in the western Pennsylvania town of Latrobe about an hour's drive east of Pittsburgh. Rogers attended Rollins College in Winter Park, Florida where he majored in music composition. Upon his graduation in 1951, Rogers was hired by NBC as an assistant producer on *The Voice of Firestone*. He later worked there as floor director for *The Lucky Strike Hit Parade*, *The Kate Smith Hour*, and the NBC *Opera Theatre*. He was married in 1952 to Joanne Byrd, a pianist and fellow Rollins graduate.

In November 1953, Rogers moved back to Pittsburgh at the request of WQED, the nation's first community-supported public television station. The station was not yet on the air, and Rogers was asked to develop a program schedule for the following year. One of the programs he developed was called *The Children's Corner*. It was a free-wheeling, live, hour-long visit with puppets and host Josie Carey, another Pittsburgher. In addition to co-producing the program, Rogers also served as puppeteer and musician. In 1955 the program series won the Sylvania Award for the best locally produced children's program in the country and remained on the air for a total of seven years.

It was on *The Children's Corner* that several regulars of today's *Mister Rogers' Neighborhood* made their first appearances—among them, Daniel Striped Tiger, King Friday XIII, X the Owl, and Lady Elaine Fairchilde.

During off-duty hours, Rogers attended both the Pittsburgh Theological Seminary and the University of Pittsburgh's Graduate School of Child Development. He was ordained as a Presbyterian minister in 1963 with a charge to continue his work with children and families through the media.

Opportunity led Rogers to Toronto later that year. There he created a children's series of fifteen-minute episodes called *Misterogers* and made his on-camera debut as the program's host. He chose to return to Pittsburgh. In 1966, at WQED, he incorporated the fifteen-minute segments into a half-hour format. The new series was distributed by the Eastern Educational Network until 1968 when it was made available for national distribution through the Public Broadcasting Service.

Also in 1968 Rogers was appointed Chairman of the Forum on Mass Media and Child Development of the White House Conference on Youth. Besides two George Foster Peabody Awards, Emmy Awards, Lifetime Achievement Awards from the National Academy of Television Arts and Sciences and from the TV Critics Association, Fred Rogers has received every major award in television for which he is eligible and many others from special-interest groups in education, communications, and early childhood. In 1999, he was inducted into the Television Hall of Fame. His life and work have been the subject of feature articles in national publications, including *LIFE*, *Reader's Digest*, *Parents*, *Esquire*, *Parade*, and *TV Guide*.

Honorary degrees have been awarded to Fred Rogers at more than 35 colleges and universities, including Yale University, Hobart and William Smith Colleges, Carnegie Mellon University, Boston University, University of Pittsburgh, North Carolina State University, University of Connecticut, and his alma mater, Rollins College.

Rogers is chairman of Family Communications, Inc., the nonprofit company that he formed in 1971 to produce

Mister Rogers' Neighborhood and that has since diversified into nonbroadcast materials that reflect the same philosophy and purpose: to encourage the healthy emotional growth of children and their families. Almost 900 episodes of *Mister Rogers' Neighborhood* have been produced. Each year, Rogers continues to add new episodes to the series, adding freshness and intimacy to what has now become the longest-running program on public television.

Fred Rogers and his wife live in Pittsburgh. They have two married sons and two grandsons.

Children may visit *Mister Rogers' Neighborhood* on the web at: www.pbs.org/rogers

About
Family Communications, Inc.

"Family Communications, Inc. is a nonprofit company dedicated to children, their families, and those who support them. Through the production of materials in all media, we encourage open and honest communication. Respect for healthy emotional, social, and intellectual development is at the core of what we do."

Family Communications, Inc. was formed in 1971 by Fred Rogers, its current chairman, to produce the national television series, *Mister Rogers' Neighborhood*, which Fred Rogers created and hosts.

The longest-running series on public television, *Mister Rogers' Neighborhood* remains the preeminent example of television's ability to communicate well with young children and their families, and to talk about and dramatize significant developmental and psychological issues.

Family Communication's work has diversified beyond broadcast television into almost all current forms of communications technology. From books for children and adults to home video, computer software to the Internet, CDs to video-based training materials, the messages that are central to Family Communications' purposes reach an ever-growing audience—an audience that encompasses children and families with special needs as well as those coping with the everyday stresses of growing and family life. Those purposes are simply expressed by Fred Rogers himself:

"For over 30 years, our 'Neighborhood' and our 'viewing neighbors' have grown in many different ways; yet, our original purpose remains: to encourage the simple and the deep in all of life, recognizing that each one of us is a unique and precious part of the world."

Visit the Family Communications, Inc. website at:
www.fci.org